SEAL PUP GROWS UP

The Story of a Harbor Seal

SMITHSONIAN OCEANIC COLLECTION

To Jennifer
— K.W.Z.

To William and Nicole
— L.B.

Book copyright © 2006, 1994 Trudy Corporation, 353 Main Avenue, Norwalk, CT 06851,
and the Smithsonian Institution, Washington, DC 20560.

Published by Soundprints Division of Trudy Corporation, Norwalk, Connecticut.

Book Design: Shields & Partners, Westport, CT

First Edition 1994
10 9
Printed in Singapore

Acknowledgements:
   Our very special thanks to Dr. Charles Handley of the department of vertebrate zoology at the Smithsonian's
National Museum of Natural History for his curatorial review, and Jack Schneider, Program Director of The Maritime
Center at Norwalk (Connecticut), for providing additional support and guidance for this book.

Library of Congress Cataloging-in-Publication Data

Zoehfeld, Kathleen Weidner.

Seal pup grows up : the story of a harbor seal / by Kathleen Weidner Zoehfeld ;
illustrated by Lisa Bonforte.
        p.   cm.
Summary: Describes how Seal Pup's mother prepares him for life on his own.
        ISBN 1-56899-026-X
1. Seals (Animals) — Juvenile fiction. [1. Seals — Fiction. 2. Animals — Infancy — Fiction.]
I. Bonforte, Lisa, ill. II. Title.
        PZ10.3.Z684 Se 1994   93-27269
        [E] — dc20   CIP
                                                                 AC

SEAL PUP GROWS UP

The Story of a Harbor Seal

by Kathleen Weidner Zoehfeld   Illustrated by Lisa Bonforte

Soundprints
Where Children Discover...

"Ma-a-a, ma-a-a!" Harbor Seal Pup crawls along the pebbly beach crying for his mother.

All around him Pup hears the calls of other seal babies. He does not pay much attention to them. He is hungry.

Not too far ahead, he sees a mother seal. He hurries to her and reaches his nose up to sniff her neck. She turns quickly and chases him away.

She is another baby's mother, not his. He moves on, crying even louder. But Pup's mother is not far away. She pushes along, trying to catch up with him.

6

It is early summer. Seal Pup's mother and several other seal mothers have given birth to their babies. They have gathered to raise their pups on this secluded beach on the coast of Maine.

The mothers follow their curious pups as they explore the rocky beach. They watch over them and do their best to keep them out of danger.

Pup's mother lumbers forward, getting closer to Pup with each push of her large body. She hears many pups crying, but she knows her own pup's cries among all the others.

When she reaches him, she sniffs his neck. His special scent tells her he is really hers. They touch noses.

Pup nuzzles her excitedly. Mother rolls over on her side and Pup begins to nurse. He drinks her rich milk.

Another mother moves near, looking for her own pup. Pup's mother raises her head and waves her front flipper, warning the other seal not to disturb them.

Once he's had his fill, Pup rests his chin on a smooth, sun-warmed rock and falls asleep — his hind flippers stretched out behind him, his front flippers out at each side.

He is a week old. His fur is a sleek gray, speckled all over with brown. From a distance, he and the other seals blend in with the shiny-smooth rocks and pebbles on the beach.

Though the pups' coloring makes them hard to see, that does not always keep them safe from enemies. A raven flies overhead and the mothers move closer to their pups.

The raven glides down to perch at the edge of a high rocky bluff behind the beach.

All the mothers look up nervously toward the bird. Pup's mother nudges him awake.

The raven circles down to the beach. He walks warily among the pups, looking for shellfish. He gets close to Pup. Too close! Mother waves her flippers frantically and chases the bird. He flutters back up to the top of the bluff.

17

Mother pushes Pup toward the water, where she knows he'll be safe. Harbor seal pups are good swimmers from birth.

The waves are lapping high on the beach. It is high tide. Pup splashes into the waves, followed by Mother. They glide swiftly through the cold, dark water.

High tide is the best time for hunting, and Mother leads Pup out to deeper waters. After following Pup around all morning, she is hungry.

She dives down and searches for a fish. Sea stars dot the bottom, but she is not interested in them.

Her large eyes help her see in the dark, murky water. Her sensitive whiskers help her feel the little ripples made by fish as they swim away.

Suddenly, a small flounder wiggles in the sand up ahead. Mother lunges after it. Her sharp teeth hold the fish fast, and she gulps it down, whole.

Pup spots a sea urchin and swims down to have a look.
He pushes at it with his nose, but the urchin's spines are prickly.
As he turns away, a loose piece of seaweed floats past his nose.
He snaps at it and carries it to the surface in his teeth. He
drops it and watches it float.

Mother darts over and snatches it. It is time to play.
Pup and his mother roll and dive. They loop through
the water and pass the little piece of kelp back
and forth between them.

As they swim, Pup nuzzles Mother's neck and tries to climb on her back. She rolls and he slides off. He tries again. This time she lets him hang on and totes him to the beach, piggyback.

When they reach the shore, Pup slides back down into the water before Mother can even turn around. She chases after him and pushes him ashore again.

She holds him firmly in place with her flipper while she checks the area for danger. The other seals seem calm. She leads Pup to their favorite resting spot, and he begins to nurse again.

Each day, for a few more weeks, Pup swims with his mother and watches her hunt.

Each day, he drinks Mother's rich milk and grows. He develops a thick layer of fat, or blubber, that will help keep him warm, even in the coldest water.

Then one day, while they are out hunting together, Pup catches his first shrimp. He likes the way it tastes. Soon he is catching fish and squid, too.

Then Mother knows it is time to bring Pup to a little cove where other youngsters his age are playing and hunting by themselves. He leaves his mother's side, eager to join the group.

Mother swims away to rejoin the main herd, but Pup does not mind. He is big and strong now. He has other pups to play with, and he knows how to catch his own food.

When autumn draws near, Pup and the other youngsters will join the main herd, too. Each day they will leave the herd and swim out in the cold Maine waters to hunt alone. When they are done, they will return to rest contentedly on their favorite beach.

About the Harbor Seal

Harbor seals live along the coastlines of the northern Atlantic and Pacific Oceans. Air-breathing mammals, harbor seals are at home both in water and on land. Using their hind flippers and streamlined bodies, they can dive to depths over 650 feet. Holding their breath for as long as 30 minutes, they scour the ocean bottom for various kinds of fish for food. Crabs, sea snails, squids, shrimp, and other marine animals are also a part of their diet.

Much less graceful on land than in water, harbor seals nevertheless must come ashore to rest and to mate. On land, they inch along on their bellies like huge caterpillars and rest together in groups at low tide. At high tide, they often swim off by themselves in search of food.

Glossary

blubber: the thick layer of fat beneath the skin of the harbor seal that helps to keep the animal warm.

bluff: a steep bank or high cliff.

flippers: a harbor seal's flat, paddle-like limbs used for propulsion and steering.

herd: a group of large animals.

kelp: a brown seaweed that grows in cold rocky coastal waters.

sea star: any of a variety of sea creatures living on coastal ocean bottoms, commonly identified by five tapered arms arranged around a central disk.

sea urchin: a ball-shaped sea creature, covered with sharp spines. Sea urchins are found on the ocean bottom in coastal areas.

Points of Interest in this Book

pp. 12-17 raven.

pp. 20-21 atlantic herring.

pp. 20-21, 28-29, 30-31 sea stars.

pp. 20-21, 22-23, 28-29, 30-31 purple sea urchin.

pp. 22-23, 28-29, 30-31 sea kelp.

pp. 28-29 scallop shell.

pp. 28-29, 30-31 silversides.

pp. 30-31 clam shell.